Weekly Reader Children's Book Club presents

SLOTH'S BIRTHDAY PARTY

DIANE REDFIELD MASSIE

Xerox Education Publications

XEROX

for Tom

Sloth's house was a terrible mess. It sat in the kapoc tree.

"I like a house that looks lived in," said Sloth. "How else can one be comfortable?" He moved the jelly jars over on his wash tub and rested his big furry feet.

"Sloth!" called Toucan outside his window. "We're all going to Rat's house for supper."

"Rat's?" said Sloth. "Rat's house is too small."

"It's a garden supper," said Toucan. "We aren't going inside."

Sloth looked out his window. "What if it rains?" he said.

"If it rains," said Toucan, "we'll go over to Armadillo's instead." She flapped her wings and flew down to Rat's front yard.

"No one ever comes to *my* house," said Sloth. He leaned on his windowsill and stared at Rat's garden.

"Are you coming?" called Rat.

"Of course I'm coming," said Sloth. A jelly jar fell out his window and landed in the vines.

"It's not right," said Sloth to himself. He rocked back and forth in his broken rocking chair. "*I* go to *their* houses. They should come to *my* house too." He looked at the calendar, hanging from his clock. "My birthday's coming up," he said, tapping his claws together. "I'll invite them all to my birthday party! They're sure to come *then*." He smiled and yawned and settled back in his chair to sleep.

By suppertime, the sky was dark. Rain drops rattled over
the leaves and bounced like beads to the ground.

"It's raining! Drat it," said Rat, looking out her door,
"and I've got the chairs out and everything!"
She hurried about, shutting her windows.

Armadillo ran through the grass. "We'd better go to my
house," he called from the yard, "where we can be inside!"

"What?" said Sloth,
waking up from his nap.
"Is it suppertime already?"

"It's raining," called Toucan. She flew past Sloth's door
and landed in the garden. "We're going to Armadillo's after
all," she said.

Sloth looked out his window. He waved to his friends below. "Why don't you all come to *my* house!" he called. "In a minute I'll have a fire going in the stove. It's nice to be inside in a storm."

"But Sloth . . ." said Rat.

"And *my* house is closer," said Sloth. He shut his window and hurried back to light the fire.

"What shall we do?" asked Rat.

Armadillo shook his shiny back. Water ran down in little streams. "Well," he said, "we *are* closer to *his* house, I suppose."

They climbed slowly up the slats that led to Sloth's front porch.

"Come in!" said Sloth, flinging open his door. It fell off its hinges and lay by the step. "What a nice night for a supper party," said Sloth, "inside a cozy, comfortable, lived-in house!"

"It was nice of you to have us," said Armadillo, looking about. "Where shall we sit?"

"You'll find the chairs somewhere," said Sloth. "They're underneath other things."

"Oh," said Rat, lifting a sheet off a box.

"Not *that*," said Sloth. "*That's* the refrigerator." He pulled down a pan, hanging from his clothesline, and hurried back to his stove.

Armadillo sat on an old rush chair. The seat was frayed and thin.

"I'll have soup ready in a moment," said Sloth. "I always have soup ready for occasions."

Toucan stared at the holes in the roof. The rain was coming through.

"It's the same soup every time," said Sloth, "but somehow it always tastes different! Sometimes it tastes stronger than at other times, depending on what's fallen in."

"*Fallen* in?" said Rat.

"You know," said Sloth. "Sometimes things get into soup you hadn't planned on."

Pitta patta pitta patta pitta patta.

Everyone listened to the rain overhead.

Plink! Plunk! Plink! Plunk! plonk! plonk! plink! plunk!

Pans and dishes lay about the room, catching the falling water.

"This roof is like a sieve!" said Toucan. Rain drops splashed on her bill.

"More like a collander," said Sloth. "There are lots of dry spots."

Plink! Plunk! Plink! Plunk! plonk! plonk! plink! plunk! Splash! sizzle! splash! sizzle! Splash! sizzle!

"Drat it!" said Sloth. "Just our luck! There's a new leak over the stove!"

"What does *that* mean?" asked Armadillo, squirming
in his chair.

"It means," said Sloth, "that the fire has gone out
and our soup will be lukewarm!"

"Lukewarm is better than cold," said Rat, hopefully.

Sloth brought out two bowls and two jelly jars.
He set them on top of the wash tub. "The jelly jars hold
more," he said, "but they don't look as nice as the bowls."
He poured the soup around. "I don't have soup spoons either,"
he added. "In fact, I only have one *big* serving spoon."

"That's all right," said Toucan. "We'll *drink* our soup."
She raised a jelly jar to her bill and swallowed.
"Well?" said Sloth. "How was it?"
"Lukewarm," said Toucan.
"Was it good?" asked Rat.
"I'm not saying," whispered Toucan.

Rat and Armadillo sipped their soup.

"Tastes like water," whispered Rat.

"Looks like the swamp," said Armadillo.

"Unfortunately," said Sloth, draining his jelly jar,
"the rain has gotten into it. It's never as good when it rains!"

"*Help!*" cried Armadillo. "*I'm stuck!*" His shell had slipped through the seat and the chair had overturned. "Help! Help!"

"Armadillo," said Sloth. "What have you done to my chair?"

"What have *I* done?!!" shouted Armadillo, crossly, "What has *it* done to me?"

"His shell is stuck," said Rat, pushing on the chair. "It won't budge."

"I can't go home like *this*!" yelled Armadillo. "Sloth will have to chop it off!"

"*Chop* my best chair?" said Sloth.

SPLASH! Water poured down on their heads from above.
"THE ROOF'S GIVING WAY!" yelled Toucan.
"HELP!" shrieked the others.

"No, it isn't," said Sloth. "It's just a big hole!
And look at the soup!" he shouted. "It's filled to the top
with water!"

"I'm going home!" said Rat, shaking water from her whiskers.

"So am I," said Toucan. "Thank you, Sloth, for the soup
and all."

"It was a lovely party," said Rat, "except for the rain."

"Lovely," said Toucan. She made swimming motions
with her wings and hurried out the door.

"WAIT FOR ME!" shouted Armadillo, crawling after them.

"You can't get down like that," said Sloth.

Armadillo stumbled on a pan. He fell against the stove. The legs and back fell off the chair, and the seat cracked down the middle.

"GOOD-BYE!" said Armadillo, waving both arms. He climbed, after Rat, down the slats on the tree to the bottom.

Sloth watched them disappear in the darkness. "They didn't like my house," he said. "They'll never come to my birthday party." He sat sadly under his umbrella by the stove until the rain had stopped.

By morning, the sun was up, warming the grass, the vines, and the trees. Sunshine sparkled on the leaves, and the puddles were steaming.

Sloth's house was damp. Sunshine came through the hole in his roof and warmed his soggy room.

Sloth made his way slowly back and forth, dumping pans of water out his window.

Rat waved from below. "Good morning, Sloth!" she called.

"My birthday's next week," said Sloth, "but I don't suppose anyone will come to my party."

"When is it?" asked Rat, hanging her towels to dry.

"On Tuesday," said Sloth. He busied himself with his empty pan and waited for Rat to answer. "Everyone's invited, of course," added Sloth. "And no one has to bring presents." He looked hopefully about, but Rat had gone inside. "I knew it!" he said. "She's not coming! None of them will come to my party." He went back to his watery work inside and tried not to think of his birthday.

On Tuesday morning, Sloth woke up early. The sun was shining in his eyes through the hole in the roof. "It's my birthday," he said. He got up slowly and stared at himself in the broken mirror above the sink.
He brushed his whiskers
and smoothed his fur.
"I'll have a party anyway,"
said Sloth, "for just me."

He found a red balloon in his drawer, next to his birthday candle, and blew it up. "I'll hang it from my clothesline," he said. It swung gently back and forth in the sunlight.

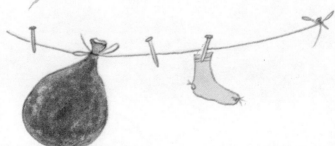

Sloth spent the morning making a cake. He frosted it with yellow frosting and lit the candle in the center. Then he sat down by his wash tub, with his serving spoon, and sang *Happy Birthday* to himself. "Happy Birthday to me! Happy Birthday to me! Happy Birthday, dear Slo-oth! Happy Birthday to me!" He made a wish and then blew out the candle.

"HAPPY BIRTHDAY, SLOTH!" shouted his friends outside.

"What?" cried Sloth. "You've come to my party?" He clapped his paws and held the cake in the air. "I haven't bitten into it yet," he said. "Wait till I get some plates!" He hurried to his cupboard and brought them out.

Three presents sat next to the wash tub.

"Presents too?" cried Sloth.

"They're useful presents," said Armadillo. "Open mine first."

Sloth pulled the lavender ribbon from Armadillo's present. Inside the paper was a chair seat, a box of screws and some glue.

"And that's not all," said Armadillo. "I'm going to fix your chairs."

"You *are*?" said Sloth. "How nice of you, Armadillo!" He opened Toucan's present next. Inside the big box were shingles and nails and a blue-handled hammer.

"I can fix my roof!" said Sloth. He tapped the shingles with the hammer and shook the box of nails.

"I'll help you," said Toucan. "We'll fix it together."

"Aren't you going to open *my* present?" asked Rat.

Sloth untied the string. "I can't believe it!" he said.
"It's four spoons and two bowls! Just what I needed!"

"Let's get to work," said Toucan.

Armadillo collected the chairs. He fastened and glued
while Rat held the pieces together.

Toucan and Sloth were pounding outside on the roof overhead.

Bang! Bang! Bang! Bang! Tap! Tap! Bang!

By late afternoon, the shingles were on and the door
and the chairs were mended.

"I wouldn't recognize my house!" said Sloth,
spreading a tablecloth over the washtub. "It's even more cozy
and comfortable than before!" He lit the candle on his cake.
"I don't have to wish again," he said. "My wish came true."

"What was it?" asked Rat.

"I wished you all were here," said Sloth, "and here you are."
He smiled at his friends and blew out the candle.

"Happy Birthday to you! Happy Birthday to you! HAPPY BIRTHDAY, DEAR SLOTH! HAPPY BIRTHDAY TO YOU!"